THE SHAPING AND RESHAPING OF EARTH'S SURFACE™

Sand, Silt, and Mud
and the Rock Cycle

Joanne Mattern

The Rosen Publishing Group's

PowerKids Press™

New York

Published in 2006 by The Rosen Publishing Group, Inc.
29 East 21st Street, New York, NY 10010

First Edition

Editor: Melissa Acevedo
Book Design: Ginny Chu

Illustration Credits: p. 6, 7 by Ginny Chu.

Photo Credits: Cover and title page, pp. 14 (top left), 20 (top right) © Royalty-Free/Corbis; p. 4 © Randy Wells/Corbis; p. 4 (top left) © Richard List/Corbis; p. 4 (top right) © Paul A. Souders/Corbis; p. 8 © Phil Schermeister/Corbis; pp. 8 (top left), 17 (top right) © The Brett Weston Archive/Corbis; p. 8 (top right) © L. Clarke/Corbis; pp. 10, 12 (bottom right) © Jeff Vanuga/Corbis; pp. 11, 14 (top right) © Ron Watts/Corbis; p. 12 (bottom left) © Galen Rowell/Corbis; p. 13 (top left) © Martin Rogers/Corbis; p. 13 (top right) © Richard Hamilton Smith/Corbis; p. 14 © David Muench/Corbis; p. 16 © Philip Gould/Corbis; p. 17 (top left) © Joe McDonald/Corbis; p. 18 © 1996 Corbis; Original image courtesy of NASA/Corbis; p. 18 (top left) © Ric Ergenbright/Corbis; p. 18 (top right) © Arne Hodalic/Corbis; p. 20 © David Papazian/Corbis; p. 20 (top left) © Pablo Corral V/Corbis.

Library of Congress Cataloging-in-Publication Data

Mattern, Joanne, 1963–
    Sand, silt, and mud and the rock cycle / Joanne Mattern.— 1st ed.
        p. cm. — (Shaping and reshaping of earth's surface)
    Includes bibliographical references and index.
    ISBN 1-4042-3197-8 (library binding)
    1. Sediments (Geology)—Juvenile literature. I. Title.

    QE471.2.M37 2006
    551.3'04—dc22
                                        2005001490

Manufactured in the United States of America

Contents

This picture shows the pinkish silt that has built up along a river in Amazonas, Venezuela.

This mud is sending off lots of steam as it boils. This picture was taken in New Zealand.

CONTENT SKILL: The Properties of Clasts

Sand is usually .04 inches (1 mm) in diameter, or width. A beach pail can hold more than three billion grains of sand!

Right:
This picture of a desert sand dune was taken in the 1990s.

Sand, Silt, and Mud: Clasts and Creators

What Are Sand, Silt, and Mud?

Earth's surface is covered with soil and rock. Over time this soil and rock breaks down to form clasts. Sand, silt, and mud are clasts that form from soil and metamorphic, sedimentary, and igneous rocks. Clasts are named for the size of the grains from which they formed. Large, coarse grains are called sand and form from small bits of rock. Sand is found mostly on beaches. Silt also forms from rock bits but is finer than sand. It is found along streams. Mud, a mixture of water and soil, is the finest of the three. It can be found anywhere. These materials are part of Earth.

Sand, silt, and mud are clasts that form from soil and metamorphic, sedimentary, and igneous rocks.

Sand, Silt, and Mud in the Rock Cycle

The rock cycle is the process by which old rocks break down to form new rocks. Sand, silt, and mud could not exist without the rock cycle, and the rock cycle could not exist without them!

The cycle begins when hot liquid magma rises to the surface of Earth. Once there it cools and hardens into igneous rocks. Through the process of weathering, igneous rocks wear down and become sand, silt, and mud. These materials mix with other matter, like dirt, to become sediment. Over time, this sediment settles into layers. Large amounts of pressure applied to the layers force

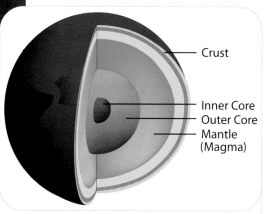

Crust

Inner Core
Outer Core
Mantle
(Magma)

The rock cycle operates through Earth's several layers. The top layer is made of rock. It is called the crust. A layer of hot liquid called magma is under the crust. Below the magma is Earth's core, which is made up of two layers. The outer layer is made up of melted metals. The inner layer is a solid metal ball.

out water and form
sedimentary rocks.
Sedimentary and
igneous rocks become
metamorphic rocks
when heat and pressure
change the minerals in
these rocks. Rocks are
forced underground

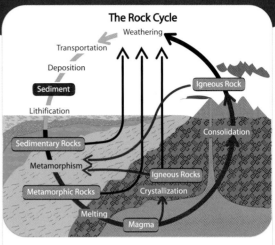

The Rock Cycle

Weathering

Transportation

Deposition

Sediment

Lithification

Sedimentary Rocks

Metamorphism

Metamorphic Rocks

Melting

Igneous Rock

Consolidation

Igneous Rocks

Crystallization

Magma

This diagram shows the rock cycle.
Sand, silt, and mud are important
parts of the rock cycle. They form
sediment, which later forms
sedimentary rocks.

through earthquakes and other natural
occurrences. Once there the rocks melt into
magma. The magma is pushed to the surface and
the rock cycle begins anew.

Sand, silt, and mud could not exist without the rock cycle,
and the rock cycle could not exist without them!

This plant root is trapped in a rock. When this happens the root weathers the rock.

Over time the ocean will wear down these Florida seashells to form sand for the beach.

CONTENT SKILL: Methods of Formation: Breakdown

Some sand is made of shells. Ocean waves break the shells into tiny pieces. In time these pieces can wear down into sand.

Right:
This picture shows the Loess Hills in Iowa. These hills have been severely eroded by wind and rain. Notice their unusual shape.

The Journey of Sand, Silt, and Mud

Breakdown of Rocks

Rocks are strong, but forces like wind and water can break them down over time to form sand, silt, or mud. One of the processes by which rocks are broken down is erosion. After the rocks are broken down, they are carried to bodies of water by forces like wind.

Weathering is another process by which rocks are broken down. Rocks stretch when they get hot and shrink when they cool. The stretching and shrinking weather the rock. Elements like oxygen can interact with a rock's minerals and change them. This is called chemical weathering.

One of the processes by which rocks are broken down is called erosion. Weathering is another process by which rocks are broken down.

9

On the Move

Broken pieces of rock and soil have a long journey before becoming sand, silt, or mud. Rain or flowing water washes the rock pieces into streams and rivers. When these streams and rivers empty into the ocean, they carry these pieces with them. As the pieces travel, they bump into each other and water rubs against them. The bumping and rubbing makes them smaller and smoother over time. They are no longer pieces of rock. They have now become either sand, silt, or mud. Different amounts and types of erosion and weathering decide which of the clasts the rock pieces will become. For example, lots of erosion forms mud's fine grains.

It takes a strong wind to move sand! The wind must be blowing at least 15 miles per hour (24 km/h) to pick up and move sand grains. The sand grains in this sand dune, which is located in Namibia, are being swept up by the wind with great force.

Once the rock pieces have become clasts, they can travel by wind. Before the rock pieces became clasts, they could only travel by water because they were too big and heavy. Now that the pieces have become clasts, they are lighter and smaller. Strong winds can pick up the tiny clasts and carry them far away. The wind rubs the clasts just as water does. This creates grains that are different from one another in size and shape. The wind then usually carries the clasts to the ocean.

This picture, taken in Oregon, shows a stream moving rocks and rock pieces. These pieces will in time form sediment and settle at the bottoms of oceans in layers.

Before the rock pieces became clasts, they could only travel by water because they were too big and heavy.

Becoming a Sedimentary Rock

What happens to the sand, silt, and mud when they reach the ocean? They sink to the bottom. The bigger, heavier grains of sand, silt, or mud fall to the bottom first. The lighter grains lay on top of them, forming layers. While forming layers, these grains mix with other material, like shells, from the ocean. This is one way clasts become sediment.

The layers of sediment are so heavy that they press down on one another. The pressure this creates forces out any water that may be trapped

Beaches are not the only places with sand. This sand is located in a desert. Its wavy patterns were created by the wind's force.

Sandstone, a sedimentary rock formed from sand, is often used to make buildings. Sandstone can be red or brown and feels rough.

Mud can be found anywhere. It can be found in forests and backyards. This mud is on a beach in Costa Rica.

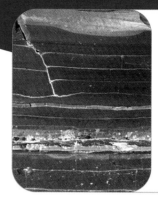

Shale, a sedimentary rock formed from mud, is used to make buildings. The layers in the rock are from sediment.

between the grains. The sand, silt, mud, and other sediment in the layers become hard. Over time these layers of sediment form sedimentary rocks. Different kinds of sediment form different types of sedimentary rocks. Sand forms a rock called sandstone. Silt forms a sedimentary rock called siltstone. Mud forms a rock called shale. Each of these rocks is used for different things. However, they are mostly used for building.

The bigger, heavier grains of sand, silt, or mud fall to the bottom first. The lighter grains lay on top of them, forming layers.

These black sand dunes are located in Quebec, Canada.

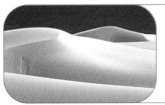
These white sand dunes can be found in New Mexico.

CONTENT SKILL: **Texture of Sand**

A sand dune is a large hill made out of sand. Some sand dunes make noises, like strange whistles or booming sounds, when the wind moves the sand around.

Right:
A mineral called quartz makes sand look tan or gray. These tan sand dunes are located in Colorado.

Texture of Sand, Silt, and Mud

Sand

Sand is made of grains that are between .0024 and .08 inches (.06 mm to 2 mm) in size. The size and texture of sand grains depends on how much erosion has occurred. A sand grain that is smooth and round has probably traveled far. This is because water and matter has rubbed against it, making it round and smooth. A grain with sharp edges has probably not traveled far.

Sand comes in many colors. The color comes from the rocks and minerals from which it is made. White sand is made from coral and shell. Black sand comes from black rocks, like obsidian.

A sand grain that is smooth and round has probably traveled very far. This is because water has rubbed against it, making it round and smooth.

Silt and Mud

Silt forms mostly through the weathering of rock pieces. It is finer than sand. Silt is so fine

These silt layers are along the banks of the Mississippi River. The silt looks thicker because it mixed in with water from the river.

that it is sometimes called rock flour. Silt grains are between .00016 to .00252 inches (.004 to .064 mm). Silt is so light and small that it is easy for water and wind to move it around. Unlike sand grains, which can be coarse and rough, silt grains always have a smooth and floury texture. Silt is often found in rivers, along the banks of streams, or in the shallow part of the ocean. Silt in the air is usually called dust.

Mud forms when soil, which is formed from weathered rock and the remains of dead plants and animals, mixes with water. It usually forms

Animals love mud. This African buffalo is covered with mud to keep insects away from his skin.

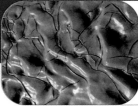

This mud is wet and has cracks in it from animals stamping through.

around bodies of water like rivers and lakes. When animals drink from a water hole or lake, they walk on the soil around the water's edges. Their feet break the soil into smaller pieces. These pieces mix with water and form a ring of mud around the hole. Mud often has bits of plant material in it along with sand or silt. This plant material has a lot of rich nutrients. Nutrients are food that living things need to live and to grow. They make mud very fertile, or good for growing things.

Silt is so light and small that it is easy for water and wind to move it around. Mud often has bits of plant material in it along with sand or silt.

This tidal flat is located in the Inner Sound at Applecross, Scotland.

Swamps are muddy places because of the amount of water mixed with soil.

Powerful storms can destroy beaches. Wind, rain, and the tide move the sand back into the ocean.

Right:
Two famous deltas are the Mississippi River delta in the Gulf of Mexico in Louisiana and the Nile River delta in Africa. This picture shows the Nile River delta.

Sand, Silt, and Mud and the Environment

Where Sand, Silt, and Mud Are Found

Sand, silt, and mud affect and change Earth's environment. Some rivers carry a large amount of sand, silt, and mud. When the river flows into the ocean, it leaves some sediment behind. The sediment can form a big fan-shaped area called a delta where the river empties into the ocean. As more sediment is left there, the delta gets larger.

Deserts can form when the wind blows large amounts of sand into a dry area. Silt can be found in places called tidal flats. Tidal flats are covered by tides that leave lots of silt behind. Mud can be found in places like swamps.

Some rivers carry a large amount of sand, silt, and mud. When the river flows into the ocean, it leaves some sediment behind.

Most children love playing with sand. When wet, sand can be formed into different shapes, like castles.

Made from sand, sandpaper is used to help make rough surfaces smoother.

The sand on the coast of Namibia, in Africa, sometimes contains diamonds. Diamonds can be used to make tools.

Right:
When sand is heated to a very high temperature, it turns into glass. Glass is used to make windows and other useful things.

The Importance of Sand, Silt, and Mud

Uses of Sand

Sand is used in many different ways. People use sand to create sandbags to keep back floodwater. Cement and bricks are made out of sand. Sand is also part of a kind of tile used to make buildings. Roofing shingles have sand in them. Glass is made mostly out of sand.

Soil that has a lot of sand is considered to be ideal for growing crops like watermelons, peanuts, and corn. Sand can also be used for play. Children on beaches play with sand by building sand castles or scooping it up in their hands. Sand has many different uses!

Cement and bricks are made out of sand. Sand is also part of a kind of tile used to make buildings.

21

Uses of Silt and Mud

Silt and mud are very useful. Silt is often added to soil to make it more fertile and to help plants grow better. Sometimes silt is added to baseball fields to create the red color we see in the infield.

Mud is also great for growing things. Because mud has so many nutrients, it is very fertile. Mud can also be used to make bricks. For thousands of years, people have cut mud into bricks and let them dry. These bricks can be used to make houses.

Sand, silt, and mud may not seem exciting, but they are an important part of the rock cycle. Without sand, silt, and mud, we would not have sedimentary rocks or any of the things we use these materials to make. Without them the rock cycle would not be able to continue. Sand, silt, and mud are an important part of our planet!

Glossary

clasts (KLASTS) Small, broken pieces of rock.

delta (DEL-tuh) A pile of sediment that collects at the mouth of a river.

earthquakes (URTH-kwayks) Shakings of Earth's surface caused by the movement of large pieces of land that run into each other.

environment (en-VY-ern-ment) All the living things and conditions of a place.

erosion (ih-ROH-zhun) The wearing away of land over time. Erosion is also the part of the rock cycle in which bits of matter become sediment.

fertile (FER-tul) Good for making and growing things.

igneous rocks (IG-nee-us ROKS) Hot, liquid, underground minerals that have cooled and hardened.

materials (muh-TEER-ee-ulz) What things are made of.

metamorphic (meh-tuh-MOR-fik) Having to do with rock that has been changed by heat and heavy weight.

minerals (MIN-rulz) Natural elements that are not animals, plants, or other living things.

sediment (SEH-deh-ment) Sand, silt, or mud carried by wind or water.

sedimentary (seh-deh-MEN-teh-ree) Having to do with layers of stones, sand, or mud that have been pressed together to form rock.

shrink (SHRINK) To make or become smaller.

temperature (TEM-pruh-cher) How hot or cold something is.

texture (TEKS-chur) How something feels when you touch it.

tidal flats (TY-dul FLATS) Land that is covered by the tide twice per day.

weathering (WEH-thur-ing) The breaking up of rock by water, wind, and chemical forces.

Index

Web Sites

Due to the changing nature of Internet links, PowerKids Press has developed an online list of Web sites related to the subject of this book. This site is updated regularly. Please use this link to access the list: www.powerkidslinks.com/sres/ssmud/